LITTLENOSE'S BIRTHDAY

Littlenose was worried – so worried that he spilt a bowl of rhinoceros soup all down the front of his furs. Father and Mother had lost his birthday stick, which was the only way they could remember the date of his birthday. And no birthday meant no birthday presents!

In this new series of stories, not only does Littlenose discover the date of his birthday, he has lots more adventures too.

Littlenose was invented for John Grant's own children, but was soon entertaining millions more when he first appeared on Jackanory in 1968.

The Neanderthal boy whose pet was bought in a mammoth sale, whose mother is in despair at the rough treatment he gives his furs, and whose exasperated father sometimes threatens to feed him to a sabre-toothed tiger, is everybody's favourite.

Besides gaining wide acceptance in Great Britain, the Littlenose stories have been translated into German, French, Italian and Japanese.

LITTLENOSE'S
BIRTHDAY

John Grant

Illustrated by the author

KNIGHT / BBC

Copyright © John Grant 1979
First published by the British Broadcasting
Corporation 1979
*This edition first published by the British Broadcasting
Corporation/Knight Books 1981*

British Library C.I.P.

Grant, John
  Littlenose's birthday.
  I. Title
  823' .914 [J]   PZ7

  ISBN 0-340-27531-6
    (0-563 20023 5 BBC)

Printed and bound in Great Britain for
Hodder and Stoughton Paperbacks,
a division of Hodder and Stoughton Ltd., Mill Road,
Dunton Green, Sevenoaks, Kent (Editorial Office:
47 Bedford Square, London, WC1 3DP) and the British
Broadcasting Corporation, 35 Marylebone High Street,
London W1M 4AA by
Richard Clay (The Chaucer Press) Ltd.,
Bungay, Suffolk

Contents

Littlenose's Birthday

Littlenose could hardly believe his ears when he heard Mother say in a worried voice, "I just can't find Littlenose's birthday stick anywhere."

It was late evening, and Littlenose was lying snuggled down under his fur bed covers and almost asleep. Mother and Father were sitting talking by the fire, and it was the mention of his name that drew Littlenose's attention.

"It can't be all that far away," said Father. "When did you have it last?"

"Littlenose's last birthday," said Mother. "Oh, dear! What are we going to do?"

"We are going to bed," said Father. "And in the morning you will wake up remembering where you put it."

Littlenose was fully awake by now. He lay in his furs and thought, "This is the greatest disaster ever." And he was not far wrong. Birthdays are very important things to most people, and the Neanderthal folk were no exceptions. The problem was that Neanderthals had no easy way of recording birthdays, or anything else, for that matter. They couldn't say that someone's birthday was on the third of August or the fourteenth of January. August and January hadn't yet been invented, so they had no calendars. Days important to the whole tribe, like the Sun Dance, were recorded on the Time Sticks with carved symbols; and when a Neanderthal child was born the Doctor fashioned a small time stick to record the event. This was the birthday stick. The birthday stick didn't actually say when a birthday was, but it did help people to work out a likely day. In any case a day or two either way rarely bothered the Neanderthal folk. Just *having* a birthday was the important thing.

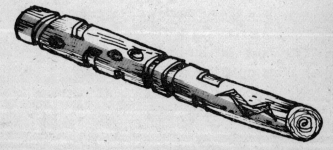

Despite what Father had said, Mother woke in the morning with still no idea where Littlenose's birthday stick could be. Littlenose was very quiet over breakfast. He was thinking, "There must be other ways of finding out when it's my birthday. I don't see why I should have to do without a birthday just because a stupid piece of wood has got itself lost."

After breakfast, he called Two-Eyes, his pet mammoth, and they sat down under his favourite tree to try to think up a solution to the problem. He tried to remember his last birthday. It seemed years ago. What had been happening at the time? What had he been doing? He decided to go for a walk to help him think. Littlenose had only walked a short distance, head bowed in thought, when he bumped hard into someone, and sat down with a thump. Rubbing his head he looked up into a ferocious mask.

It was the Doctor. He was also tribal magician, and Littlenose gulped. He'll turn me into a frog, he thought in terror.

Then the Doctor held out a hand to help him to his feet. "Sorry about that, lad," he said in a kindly voice from behind his mask. "Wasn't watching where I was going. Would you awfully mind giving me a hand with these?" And he started to gather up a number of skin-wrapped parcels which he had dropped.

Relieved not to be a frog, Littlenose followed the

Doctor, a parcel under each arm. The Doctor was evidently in a chatty mood. "Seen anything of that crazy uncle of yours, lately?" he asked.

"Uncle Redhead?" said Littlenose.

"That's him," said the Doctor. "Good friend of mine. Usually brings me something useful from his travels. Last time it was yellow bogweed. I use it a lot. It has just the right nasty taste that all good medicine should have."

The Doctor went on to talk of other things, but Littlenose was no longer listening. His mind was racing back to that particular visit of Uncle Redhead's. That had been just before his birthday. Uncle Redhead had brought him a present (not to be opened until his birthday) of a set of fire-making flints. He remembered that because he had tried them out on the morning of his birthday and had set the bed clothes alight! At his cave, the Doctor thanked Littlenose for his help and gave him an apple. Then, back under his tree, Littlenose set to thinking again.

The yellow bogweed grew far away. It had to be picked when it was in flower in late summer, so it must have been early autumn when Uncle Redhead had made his visit. Well, that was a start. His birthday must be sometime in the early autumn.

It was by now dinner time, so he went home. While he ate, he continued to think about his birthday, until Mother shouted, "For goodness sake, Littlenose!

Watch what you're doing. You'll have your dinner all over you if you don't pay attention." But he wasn't listening. He absent-mindedly lifted his bowl of rhinoceros soup, and somehow it ended in a hot, greasy mass all down the front of his furs.

Father took him by the ear and ran him out of the cave. "Don't come back until you've got that mess cleaned off," he shouted.

"It'll probably mean a new pair of furs," said Mother. And Littlenose perked up his ears at that. Mother didn't say any more. But that was enough. Father had taken Littlenose to the market for new furs not long before his last birthday, and he remembered something special about the journey. Father had met several old friends at the market, and had spent so long reminiscing with them about old times that they were late leaving for home. They had been overtaken by darkness. Father, as usual, said it was all Littlenose's fault for dawdling. But Littlenose remembered that there had been a full moon in a cloudless sky to light their way home. So that meant that his birthday was not long after a full moon some time in early autumn.

Getting his furs as clean as he could, he went back to his favourite tree to do some calculations. Sums were not a Neanderthal speciality. In a land where the good things of life tended to be in short supply, counting usually went no further than: one, two . . . plenty. But Littlenose had to be sure how long after the full moon his birthday was. He cast his mind back, carefully ticking off the days on his fingers.

The day after he had been to market had been spent chopping firewood for Mother. And the day after that he had tied the firewood into bundles and stacked them in the cave. That was two days. Was the next his birthday? No. He remembered that day because it had poured with rain, and Mother had blamed him because Two-Eyes had wandered into the cave dripping water everywhere from his fur. He also remembered Mother threatening that there would be no birthday for him if there was any more of his nonsense. That was three days accounted for.

By now it was almost supper time, so Littlenose ran home. This time, he kept his thinking for after the meal. And it was just as well that he was paying attention, for Mother said to him, "You've to go over to Auntie's cave tomorrow. She wants someone to help with her cleaning, and I said that you would be glad to." Littlenose wasn't too pleased with this news. Cleaning someone else's cave was bad enough, but Littlenose was just a bit afraid of Auntie. She wasn't Littlenose's aunt, of course. That was what

everyone called her. She was rather a strange old lady
who lived in a cave some distance from the others.
The cave was a mysterious clutter of strange objects,
in the middle of which Auntie was usually to be found
stirring some strange-smelling brew over a fire. She
made medicine, much to the annoyance of the
Doctor. And a lot of people preferred it, to his even
greater annoyance.

Littlenose arrived at Auntie's cave next morning, to find her standing outside, leaning on a stick. As soon as she saw him, she said, "Come along! There's no time to waste," and walked *away* from the cave and into the woods.

"I thought we were going to tidy your cave," said Littlenose.

"First things first," said Auntie. "Can you climb trees?"

Littlenose wondered if he should run away while he had the chance, but instead he found himself saying, "Yes."

"Good," said Auntie. "Becaase I want you to rescue Greywing."

"I see," said Littlenose, although he didn't really.

It was very tiring walking with Auntie. On one side she leaned on a stick, and on the other she leaned on Littlenose. Although the old lady looked small and frail, she was heavy. They stopped under a tree, and Auntie said: "Well, here we are." She looked up and called, "All right, Greywing, my pet. Auntie's here."

To Littlenose's astonishment a strange, croaking voice came from the tree. "Auntie! Auntie!" Then there was a sort of crazy giggle. Littlenose looked up, and found himself staring at a decidedly scruffy, and remarkably stupid-looking jackdaw.

"Well, don't just stand there," said Auntie. "Climb up and bring him down."

"But he's a bird. Why can't he fly down?"

"He broke his wing as a chick," said Auntie. "He never learned to fly. But he's very good at climbing. Up, that is. How to get down tends to baffle him."

Littlenose took a deep breath and started to climb. It wasn't difficult, and in a few moments he was astride the branch where Greywing sat watching him with a suspicious as well as a stupid look. Littlenose stretched out a hand towards the jackdaw and said, "Come on, Greywing. Good bird." Greywing hopped along the branch away from Littlenose. "Don't be silly," said Littlenose. "I've come to get you down." Greywing gave a sort of squawk and looked down towards the ground.

"Hurry up," called Auntie's voice from below. "I haven't got all day."

"I'm doing my best," muttered Littlenose to himself, as he started inching his way along the branch towards Greywing. Greywing watched him for a moment, then sidled farther away again. "How am I supposed to help you if you keep doing that," said Littlenose in exasperation. "You're even stupider than you look." The branch was beginning to bend in an alarming way as Littlenose (and Greywing) moved closer to the end. Again Littlenose reached out a hand. And this time Greywing didn't back off. Instead, he pecked at Littlenose's finger. That was too much. With a yell, Littlenose made a grab at the bird, lost his balance, and fell off the branch. The foliage broke his fall, but he still hit the ground with a hard thump, his hair full of leaves, and a very angry jackdaw clutched in one hand.

"You might have been more careful," said Auntie, as she settled a peevish-looking Greywing on her shoulder. "He could have hurt himself. He's a very delicate bird." Greywing croaked "Auntie" a couple of times, then appeared to fall asleep.

They made their way back to Auntie's cave. "It's too near dinner time to start now," she said. "Come back this afternoon and we'll get on with the cleaning."

It was only after he had limped home and was eating his dinner that Littlenose began to think about his birthday again. Before he returned to Auntie he took a piece of soft stone, and on the cave wall above his bed he noted what he had found out so far. He drew a circle to represent a full moon, and next to it three dots to represent the three days he had accounted for so far, like this:

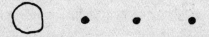

But what had happened on the fourth day? He was coming out of the cave when it came back to him in a flash. The fire! The burning bed clothes! He remembered Father rushing them outside and putting out the flames in a large puddle left from the day before. And the fire had started because he was sitting in bed trying out his new flints. The birthday present from Uncle Redhead. He rushed back into the cave and added another mark for the fourth day. His birthday!

Tidying Auntie's cave was a rather strange experience. To begin with, Auntie's idea of tidying appeared to be to move everything in the cave around a bit, frequently back into its original place. Also, the contents of the cave were different, to say the least. There were bowls, bags, bundles and just plain heaps of strange substances. Curious objects of all sorts lay in corners, along ledges, and piled on the floor. There was dust everywhere. Not ordinary dust, but dust that came in strange colours and gave off even stranger perfumes. Littlenose sneezed and blinked his way through the afternoon carrying and dragging things about the cave, while Auntie sat by the fire and directed operations by waving her stick at him. At last the job was done.

Littlenose, with a weary sigh, sat down to rest, and to his surprise Auntie produced apples, nuts and honey. "I know all about boys and their stomachs," she said. "You've been here before, haven't you?" Littlenose remembered Mother dragging him to see Auntie about a fearful purple rash he had. Auntie had evidently forgotten that the rash had turned out to be elderberry juice, which had washed off, to Mother's great embarrassment. "Yes," Auntie went on, "it was the essence of sagewort that cured you. Freshly picked in the light of the second full moon after the first foxglove. . . ." She rambled on, but Littlenose wasn't listening. He thanked her for the apples, nuts and honey, and ran all the way home. He took the piece of soft stone and completed the picture on the cave wall above his bed:

He had remembered that the elderberry incident had been several weeks before his last birthday. He couldn't remember a full moon, but Auntie had said that the sagewort was freshly picked in the full of the moon. He did some more figuring, and had just reached an exciting conclusion when Mother and Father came in. Mother was speaking to Father. "Thank goodness I've found it," she said. "The fourth day after . . ."

"I know," Littlenose interrupted her. "The fourth day after the third full moon after the first foxglove. And tomorrow's my birthday."

"How did you know?" gasped Mother.

"I just did," said Littlenose.

"That boy is going to be too clever for his own good one of these days," said Father, darkly.

But Littlenose didn't care. Tomorrow was his birthday, and he went off to bed to dream about all the wonderful presents he expected to get.

The Juniper Cousins

Littlenose heard Father shouting long before he reached the cave. There was nothing new in Father's shouting, but this sounded different. "Probably something *I've* done," thought Littlenose, and he crept towards the cave entrance, trying to catch what Father was shouting about.

"But it's only a one-apartment cave," Father shouted again. "How can it possibly hold eight people? Why did you invite them in the first place?"

"We owe them a visit," came Mother's voice. "They were very hospitable when we visited them in the mountains. It's the least we can do."

Now Littlenose understood. His Uncle Juniper and his whole family were coming to stay. Uncle Juniper lived many days' journey away in the high

20

mountains, where he gathered the berries of the juniper bushes for a living. Juniper berries were highly prized by the Neanderthal folk for making medicine, and every autumn Uncle Juniper came down from the mountains to sell his fruit at the market. He was really very famous, but because he lived so far away very few people had actually met him.

Mother spoke again. "Nosey's wife told me that her husband had met Juniper at the market, and that he had his whole family with him. So I sent a message asking them to stay for a few days."

Littlenose recalled his holiday in the mountains. Uncle Juniper had three boys, who were, of course, Littlenose's cousins. But then, the Juniper family lived in a spacious two-apartment cave with plenty of room for visitors. He began to understand why Father had been shouting. The Junipers lived by themselves, with no neighbours nearer than the other side of the mountains. They were simple people, and Father unkindly called them Country Bumpkins, Hillbillies and Yokels. Still, it would mean someone new to play with, and Littlenose began to look forward to his cousins' arrival.

The Juniper family arrived late one afternoon a few days later. Littlenose shook hands with his Uncle, kissed his Aunt and turned to greet the boys.

"Hi, there, Littlenose," said the biggest cousin, giving Littlenose a rather too hearty thump on the back. "How does a mammoth get down from an oak tree?"

"Eh?" said Littlenose, still trying to get his breath.

"Sits on a leaf and waits for autumn," said the cousin. And the three of them shrieked with laughter, nudging each other and Littlenose and generally falling about.

"I suppose that's meant to be funny," thought Littlenose.

It was the same during the evening meal. The grown-ups were so busy talking among themselves that they paid no attention to the boys, and Littlenose found it difficult to get on with the important business of eating. First one, then another of the Juniper boys nudged him and whispered things like: "Why do mammoths never forget? Because no one ever tells them anything!" and: "What do you call a deaf mammoth? Anything you like; it can't hear you!"

Littlenose tried to edge away out of earshot, then Mother looked up and said, "For goodness sake, sit still and don't fidget. Look at your cousins! They're behaving themselves!"

At last it was bedtime, and Littlenose hoped that a good night's sleep might help things. But not a bit of it. The cousins giggled and whispered in the dark more of their stupid mammoth jokes, and when Littlenose said, "Please be quiet and let me get some sleep," Father shouted, "Be quiet, Littlenose; you'll wake your cousins." It was all very unfair!

At breakfast, Littlenose decided that the best thing was to ignore the Juniper boys, even when they leaned right over and whispered in his ear, "How do mammoths catch squirrels?" He just looked straight in front and waited for Mother to serve breakfast.

"Don't be so rude to your guests, Littlenose," said Father. "Answer them when they speak to you."

Littlenose sighed at the great injustice of it all, but decided to say nothing, and had just started to eat when the smallest cousin said: "Look, Littlenose! Over there."

Heeding Father's words, Littlenose looked, but could see nothing remarkable.

"Oh, it's gone," said the cousin, and Littlenose went back to his breakfast. It seemed to have an odd flavour, but he was hungry and tucked in just the same. The cousins were eating more slowly, and seemed more interested in watching him than in eating. The taste grew stronger the farther he got down his clay bowl. And when he reached the dead frog at the bottom he knew why. He also knew who had put it there. But before he could do anything about it, Mother chased the boys outside to play while she cleared up.

Two-Eyes, who had been made to sleep outside to make room for the visitors, came running up to Littlenose. Jumping on the little mammoth's back, Littlenose said: "Come on, Two-Eyes, let's go somewhere for a quiet think." And leaving his

24

Juniper cousins to their own devices, they galloped
away into the woods.

The first quiet thought that Littlenose had was to
run away from home, at least until the visitors had
gone. But his second thought was that it would be
easier to keep out of their way as much as possible.
Having made up his mind, he went back to the caves.
A lady called from one of them, "Hello, Littlenose.
How are you today?"

"Fine, thank you," said Littlenose.

He was about to strike up a conversation when the lady stooped down and said, "I wonder who could have left this?" A large skin-wrapped parcel was lying by the cave entrance. She was just about to pick it up when the parcel gave a leap and bounced along the ground to disappear into a clump of bushes. At the last moment Littlenose saw the string and heard an unmistakable giggle. The lady had sat down with a thump and was shrieking her head off. People came running from the other caves. "It was that terrible boy," she cried, pointing at Littlenose. "Playing tricks like that! It shouldn't be allowed! It isn't good for people, that sort of thing!"

Littlenose tried to explain, but no one would listen. The cousins, meanwhile, stood at the back of the crowd, grinning all over their faces.

Littlenose arrived home to a stern talk from Father on the subject of annoying the neighbours. It was made even worse by Father's insisting on referring to the cousins as perfect examples of Neanderthal boyhood. The evening meal was a repeat of the previous one, except that the supply of mammoth jokes had apparently run out and the cousins kept up a running stream of equally unfunny jokes about sabre-tooth tigers.

At last it was bedtime. With eight people it was a bit of a squash in the cave, but Littlenose had managed to keep his fur bed covers just a bit separate from the others. With a sigh of relief at the end of a pretty miserable day, he slid down beneath the covers. Next moment he was leaping around holding his foot and yelling at the top of his voice. "Something bit me!"

Everyone came running, Father pulled back the bedclothes . . . and the angry-looking hedgehog which had been trying to find a way out since the cousins had put it in earlier, scuttled into a corner and rolled into a ball. Father was furious. "You know the rules about pets," he shouted. "You're lucky I let Two-Eyes into the cave. Now, get that creature out at once." But the creature, guessing that it was not exactly welcome, and needing some fresh air anyway, had unrolled and vanished into the night.

Littlenose lay awake that night wishing he had
decided to leave home after all. After breakfast next
morning he went off and sat under his favourite tree,
where he did most of his more important thinking.
He was quite alone, having managed to give the
cousins the slip, while Two-Eyes had gone off on
some business of his own. Littlenose considered all
sorts of attractive schemes for getting his own back.

For instance, he knew of a cave in the forest which
was the home of a particularly evil-tempered black
bear. Supposing he could trick his cousins into

thinking that there was some special treat in the cave
. . .! There would be . . . for the bear! Perhaps he
might lure them on to a floating log in the river and
send them sailing all the way to the sea? Oh, dear,
why did all the best ideas have to be the most difficult
to put into practice? His daydreams were shattered
by a sudden noise. Sudden noises usually spelled
danger in those days, and Littlenose was about to
take to his heels when he recognised something in the
noise. It was a squeal, like that given by a small and
frightened mammoth. Littlenose jumped to his feet.
The squealing was coming closer, but it was
accompanied by a strange jangling and clattering.

The bushes parted, and Two-Eyes burst through, his eyes wide with terror. He was desperately trying to get away from a clattering collection of broken pots and old bones which came bouncing out of the bushes behind him, attached by a long string to his tail. There was no need to ask who had put them there. Two-Eyes ran to Littlenose, and in a moment the string was untied and the little mammoth sank breathless to the grass.

This was going too far! Playing tricks on Littlenose and even Neanderthal ladies was one thing, but to frighten a poor harmless creature like Two-Eyes was too much. Littlenose, of course, conveniently forgot that he spent more time playing tricks on Two-Eyes than anything else. He would have his revenge if it was the last thing he did.

And, strangely, that very afternoon he got the inkling of a plan.

When Littlenose and Two-Eyes returned to the cave they found that the Juniper boys were still out, but that the grown-ups were sitting around the fire talking. Father was saying, "Yes, the Old Man, the leader of our tribe, is anxious to meet you. He's asked me to invite you on his behalf to a reception tomorrow. I'll warn you now, he fancies himself at making speeches and you're likely to be bored to tears. But he usually lays on a good spread at those sort of things."

"What about the boys?" asked Uncle Juniper.

"Oh, they can come in time for the food," said Father. "We'll leave Littlenose with them. He knows where the place is."

Littlenose sat in his own special corner of the cave and hugged himself with delight. If he could work things right, he would have a magnificent revenge for himself, Two-Eyes and the neighbour lady. That evening, he sat with his cousins outside the cave chatting about this and that, and listening to more terrible jokes. During a lull in the conversation, he looked up and said with a sigh, "Well, I'm certainly glad it isn't me."

33

"What do you mean?" asked the oldest cousin.

"Surely they've told you," said Littlenose. "You've been chosen to be presented to the Old Man."

"What of it?" said the cousin.

"Ah, now I understand," said Littlenose. "They probably didn't want to worry you. I don't blame them. People have been known to run away from home to avoid being presented. I was scared stiff, I don't mind telling you, when it was my turn. That was when the Old Man gave me my special spear." Littlenose neglected to say that the presentation of the spear had been the result of a considerable misunderstanding, but that's another story.

The cousins were leaning forward now, eager to hear more. And Littlenose didn't disappoint them. "Listen carefully," he said. "This is very important." And Littlenose told them such a convincing story that by the time he had finished even he was almost believing it.

"The Old Man," he said, "is leader of the tribe, and to be presented to him is a great honour. But it isn't easy. Leaders of tribes aren't like ordinary men. That's why they're leaders. They are proud and fierce, with strange powers. Why, it's said that the Old Man can stop a charging rhinoceros with one glance. It's his eyes, you see, which are to be feared. No one has ever looked him straight in the eye and lived to tell of it! You will be presented to the Old Man tomorrow in the presence of the whole tribe; and because I have already done it, I have been entrusted with seeing that you get everything right. Because, if you don't . . ." Littlenose paused dramatically, and the cousins sat with mouths open in wonder. "No wonder," thought Littlenose, "that Father calls them 'simple country folk'."

Before setting out for the Old Man's reception the

next day, Father took Littlenose to one side. "You'd only be bored with the grown-up chat," he said. "Bring the boys when the shadow reaches the pebble." And he stuck a twig in the ground so that it cast a long shadow in the sunlight, and placed a pebble a little way ahead of the shadow.

As soon as the grown-ups had gone, Littlenose turned to his cousins and said, "Right. Time to get ready! Remember what I said about the mud. It's to show that you are truly *humble* in the presence of the Old Man. And don't forget how you approach him. On no account must you look directly at his face." The cousins disappeared outside, and Littlenose quickly moved the pebble a little farther from the twig's shadow. The cousins returned and started smearing handfuls of mud on themselves. A ring round each eye. Patches on each cheek. A dab on the nose. And rings and dots on arms, legs and bodies. Littlenose could hardly believe that they were actually doing it. The shadow had reached the spot which Father had marked with the pebble. "I must go on ahead, now," said Littlenose. "Follow me when the shadow reaches the pebble."

The grown-ups were gathered in the sunshine outside the Old Man's cave when Littlenose came wandering up looking very downcast. "Where are the boys?" asked Uncle Juniper.

"Oh, they're messing about with mud and stuff," said Littlenose.

36

At that moment, a gasp went up from the assembled guests as three strange figures appeared. They were crawling on hands and knees . . . backwards. Slowly they approached the Old Man, who said, "Well, bless my soul! What funny people." Someone tittered. "Stand up and let me see you," said the Old Man. They stood up, but with eyes shut tight, and the laughter grew at the weird spectacle of three boys covered in splodges of mud, eyes shut, and trembling with terror. Uncle Juniper wasn't laughing, however. "One of your local customs?" said the Old Man, turning to him.

Instead of replying, Uncle Juniper grabbed at the boys, and cuffed their ears, while they yelled, "But we thought . . ." And the whole tribe laughed and laughed, but no one laughed louder than Littlenose—unless it was the lady neighbour.

That was the end of the visit. With the boys gone, Littlenose relaxed again, and was soon happily playing tricks on Two-Eyes as was, after all, only proper.

Littlenose the Decoy

Being clever in Littlenose's day was almost regarded as a crime. No one really minded the occasional good idea, but for a Neanderthal man to be good at too many things was regarded by the other members of the tribe with considerable suspicion. Littlenose's Uncle Redhead was incredibly clever, and consequently looked upon very suspiciously indeed. He wasn't actually a member of Littlenose's tribe, but from time to time dropped in on a short visit. He usually had a surprise for Littlenose, and this time it was the strangest to date. The family were sitting round the fire after the evening meal chatting, when Uncle Redhead reached over to his pack and rummaged for a moment. Then he handed something to Littlenose. "I picked this up from one of the southern tribes," he said.

Littlenose held the strange object up to the firelight. "It's a duck," he exclaimed. "A toy duck." And he tried to keep the disappointment out of his voice.

"Not a toy duck," said Uncle Readhead. "This is one of the cleverest pieces of hunting gear I've ever seen."

"Well, it certainly can't fly away," said Father. "It's made out of twigs. I wouldn't want to eat it."

"Well you wouldn't have to pluck it," said Mother, brightly. "It hasn't any feathers."

Uncle Redhead gave Mother a patient look, and went on. "It's what they call a decoy. What you do is set it afloat on a pond or a smooth part of the river. Then you hide nearby with your spear ready. Some ducks come flying along, and they see your duck and think it must be feeding, and come down to join it. Then, you've got them. It's easy."

Father fell about, laughing. "This is too much," he cried. "Ducks aren't completely stupid. Or are they? Or blind?"

"It *works*," said Uncle Redhead in a slightly huffy tone. Father was going to say more, but Mother tactfully changed the subject by telling Littlenose that it was his bedtime.

Littlenose lay in bed that night and thought about the imitation duck. The fact that Father didn't think much of it didn't mean a thing. If Uncle Redhead said something worked, then it did.

Next morning after breakfast, Littlenose set off with his boy-size spear in one hand, and the decoy duck tucked under his arm. He made his way to a large and rather gloomy pond near the edge of the forest. Kneeling carefully by the water's edge he launched the imitation duck, which drifted, slightly lop-sided, away from the bank. Then he hid in a handy clump of willows and waited, spear at the ready.

He waited and waited, but nothing happened.
Midges bit him. Caterpillars dropped from the leaves
on long silky threads into his hair, and the occasional
frog plopped into the water, but there was not a duck
in sight. He was just deciding to go home when he
heard a sound from overhead. He saw nothing at
first, but the sound came quickly closer. A loud
quacking. Then a pair of duck came into view,
winging swiftly across the tree-tops towards the river.
Littlenose thought that at least one of them glanced
down towards the pond where his decoy bobbed on
the ripples in a most realistic manner, but they didn't
stop, and were soon lost to view. That was that, he
decided. Might as well go home.

What Littlenose didn't know was that the gloomy pond was the home of a very large and very old pike. It was the terror of the perch and minnows with which it shared its kingdom, and when it wasn't feeding on them the pike liked nothing better than a tasty bird. Adult birds were too quick, but many a young moorhen or mallard had been gulped from below as it paddled after its mother. Today the pike could hardly believe its luck. For on the surface of the water, silhouetted against the sky, was the shape of an adult duck. Without hesitation the great fish launched itself upwards, its huge jaws wide open.

Littlenose had just found a long branch with which to retrieve the decoy and was reaching over the water towards it when he almost fell in with fright. The water boiled up suddenly in white foam. He had a momentary glimpse of huge jaws, and the decoy was gone, save for the odd fragment of broken twig. A moment later the decoy, looking a bit chewed, bobbed to the surface as the pike disgustedly spat it out and swam off in a bad temper to its hole under the bank.

Littlenose went home carrying the soggy mass of woven twigs, now hardly recognisable as a duck. The decoy *had* been a success after a fashion, even though he hadn't caught any ducks. Then he put it away in his own special corner of the cave and forgot all about it.

It was several weeks later that Father came home in a great state of excitement. A herd of bison had been reported nearby, and a hunt was being organised. "I hope we're luckier this time," said Father as he got his hunting spear ready.

Hunting bison was one of the most difficult things undertaken by the Neanderthal folk. It wasn't because bison were difficult to see – they were enormous. Nor was it because they were scarce. Far

from it. The great bison herds numbered thousands of animals at a time, and were slow-moving; ambling along, grazing as they went. Bison were just extremely wary. If a hunter approached a grazing herd, the animals, without appearing even to look up, moved away from him, so that he never got any closer, no matter how hard he tried. If the hunter were hasty, then the herd would stop grazing and start to trot out of reach, and at the very worst they might stampede at a wild gallop and be gone in a thunder of hooves and a cloud of dust. The only hope for a Neanderthal hunting party was to catch an old or sick or stupid animal that had strayed from the herd. Even that was dangerous, because if a bison *didn't* retreat it was as ferocious as anything on four legs.

And it was no different this time. The hunters came home tired and empty-handed, and muttering in the direction of a particular hunter called Nosey. Nosey had come up with the bright idea of luring a straggler from the herd by making a noise like a bison in distress. They had hidden at the edge of the woods while Nosey mooed and bellowed for all he was worth. It didn't fool the bison for a moment, but it *did* fool a passing sabre-tooth tiger, which leapt in the direction of the sound, and was astonished when instead of a bison a dozen terrified Neanderthal hunters ran yelling in all directions. Luckily the tiger was too amazed to give chase!

46

Littlenose stood at the back of the crowd and listened. The idea of Nosey's trying to sound like a bison had set him thinking. It might have worked, he thought, if Nosey had *looked* like a bison. Maybe one that had found a particularly tasty patch of grass. In other words, if they had used a decoy, like the one Uncle Redhead had given him. A bison decoy instead of a duck!

He mentioned the idea to Father just as he was going to bed. Father didn't answer right away. He couldn't. He was helpless with laughter. Eventually he wiped the tears from his eyes and gasped: "Oh, what would we do without you, Littlenose? That's the first laugh I've had in a whole miserable day. Ho! Ho! Ho!"

"I'm serious," said Littlenose.

"Don't spoil it," shouted Father. And he roared with laughter again. Littlenose pulled the fur bedclothes over his ears and made up his mind to speak to someone sensible in the morning.

The first person Littlenose met after breakfast was Nosey. Nosey was well-known for his fantastic ability to track animals by scent alone with his exceptionally handsome nose. Now he was in disgrace. No one would speak to him unless it was to make unkind remarks about his animal imitations, and he was pleased when Littlenose came up and said, "Mr Nosey, I've got a good idea, but Father won't listen. He just laughs."

"Well," replied Nosey, "I could do with a few good ideas, if I'm going to live down yesterday's little episode! Tell me all about it."

And Littlenose told Nosey about Uncle Redhead's decoy. He brought out the battered bundle of woven twigs that still managed to look faintly like a duck. "Given a chance," he said, "it would easily have deceived a duck. It certainly deceived the pike."

"I know how you feel," said Nosey, "but how is this going to help catch a bison? They have very little to do with ducks, to the best of my knowledge."

"We make a bison decoy," said Littlenose, "out of branches and old scraps of skin and fur. We put it near where the bison are grazing, and the hunters lie in wait nearby. Let's go and tell them."

"Not so fast," said Nosey. "We want to see if it works first; and in any case no one will go hunting with me now. But come to my cave. I have a great pile of odds and ends of fur and we'll see what can be made of it."

49

All this time, a new hunting party had been getting ready to set out for another attempt upon the bison herd. It was smaller than the previous day's, as most of the hunters said that it was a waste of time. "It'll be a different story when it comes to sharing out the meat," the hunting party muttered darkly, shouldering their spears and setting off trying to look more hopeful than they felt.

Littlenose and Nosey's imitation bison could only be described one way. It was a work of art! They stood outside Nosey's cave and glowed with pride at their handiwork. Nosey's cave was somewhat separate from the other caves, so that no one spied on them as they fetched branches from the forest and tied and twisted them into a rough framework. Four stout boughs made the legs, and the rest was covered with a shaggy patchwork of discarded furs, efficiently, if not very expertly, sewn together. Two specially selected branches had been peeled white and whittled. Tied on the head they made a most impressive pair of bison horns.

"Well, that's that," said Nosey. "Let's try it out."
Taking a pair of legs each, they heaved the decoy off
the ground and set off by a back route away from the
caves towards where the bison had last been. The
herd was still there. It wasn't all that far, but Nosey
and Littlenose collapsed in the shelter of a clump of
trees and gasped for breath. The decoy seemed as
heavy as a real bison, while the dust from the old
skins got in their eyes and up their noses. They
watched the quietly grazing herd. It stretched out of
sight on either hand, looking neither to left nor right.
But they mustn't waste time, and getting stiffly to
their feet, they began dragging the decoy towards the
unsuspecting bison. And that was the problem. The
bison were so unsuspecting that they didn't even look
up. Nosey and Littlenose chose a likely spot and
propped the dummy in position. Then, they hid and
waited. And waited. And waited some more.

"It's too far away," said Nosey. "We'll have to move it closer." Once again they hoisted the decoy on to their shoulders. They had found that the only way to carry it was to get right under the skins and take a leg over each shoulder. They could just see out through odd gaps in their rough sewing, but spent more time looking at their feet to avoid tufts and tussocks.

At length Littlenose panted, "This will have to do. I can't carry it another step."

They set it down carefully, making sure that the legs were firmly on the ground. Then Nosey, who was at the front end, looked out and said, "We're very close. Surely one of them will notice. Come on, Littlenose. Let's slip away and see what happens."

But Littlenose had been looking out too. "It's too late," he said.

A large bull bison had stopped grazing and was
standing stock still gazing steadily at the decoy. Then
it stepped out from the ranks of the herd. It sniffed the
air and swung its head from side to side.

"I don't like the look of this," said Littlenose.

"It's all right," said Nosey. "Probably just wants
to be friendly. If we pretend we're grazing it might
come closer." And he pushed the head of the decoy
down towards the grass, at the same time making his
now well-known bison imitation.

The bull continued to watch. Unfortunately, it
didn't see a friendly bison quietly eating grass. It saw
a strange bison standing in a very menacing manner.
It saw the strange bison suddenly put its head down
and shake its horns in a decidedly provocative way,
and at the same time making threatening noises deep
in its throat.

The bull took a step forward. Then another. "It's coming," said Nosey.

The bull stopped, and began pawing ground, meanwhile lowering its head and shaking *its* horns. "I think we've been here long enough," said Nosey. "Move slowly and calmly, and we'll be all right." They hoisted the legs of the decoy once more on to their shoulders and slowly began the long walk back to the shelter of the trees. Behind, unseen, the bull bison followed at a walk. Then the walk became a trot, and Nosey cried, "Hurry, Littlenose!"

But Littlenose had felt the tremble in the hard ground as the bison broke into a gallop, and he ran. He overtook Nosey, so that the bison suddenly saw its rival's back legs running past its front ones, while an angry voice shouted; "Come back, Littlenose. It doesn't look natural!"

"I don't care," cried Littlenose. 'I'm getting out." And he scrambled from under the decoy and ran, closely followed by Nosey.

Charging down on its fallen rival, the bison ripped into the decoy with its horns, while Littlenose and Nosey watched, horrified, from behind a tree.

Suddenly, Littlenose and Nosey were pushed aside. A crowd of men came rushing out from among the trees. It was the hunting party! And the bison never saw them as it trampled the last of the decoy into the dust. In a moment they were on it with their spears.

The Neanderthal folk held a party that night, and
Littlenose and Nosey were guests of honour. As
always, the Old Man made a speech. In his speech
the Old Man praised Littlenose and Nosey, and said
that he wanted this whole decoy business looked into
further. But Littlenose was barely listening. He had
reluctantly to agree with Father that you could have
too much of a good idea. Then he got on with the
more important business of stuffing himself with as
much bison meat as he could.

Littlenose's Friend

Littlenose was often lonely. The other boys of the tribe laughed and made fun of him because of the berry-sized nose which gave him his name. They all had large, snuffly Neanderthal noses. So, most of the time he played by himself, or with Two-Eyes.

One day Littlenose sat under his favourite tree thinking out loud, while Two-Eyes sat nearby thinking quietly. "If I had a friend," Littlenose said, "I would be the happiest boy in the world. We would do all sorts of marvellous things together. You'd like that, too, wouldn't you, Two-Eyes?"

Two-Eyes wasn't sure. Even *one* of Littlenose was more than he could cope with at times.

"Or a brother," went on Littlenose. "That would be even better, because he would live with us in the

cave and we could play all the time. *And*, what's
more, there would be two of us to do all the fetching
and carrying that I do for Mother and Father. It's
very hard work being an only child, Two-Eyes." But
Two-Eyes had fallen asleep and said nothing.

A few days later, Mother announced that she
intended to start spring cleaning the cave after
breakfast. Littlenose knew what that meant. There
would be even more fetching and carrying than
usual, and he didn't fancy being around any more
than he had to. He decided there and then to go for a
picnic. A bit of quiet larder-raiding produced some
cold meat, a couple of apples and a piece of
honeycomb. He put these into his hunting bag,
whistled to Two-Eyes, and set off over the hill behind
the cave.

By the time the caves were out of sight, Littlenose was feeling quite cheerful. It was a beautiful spring day. He laughed and shouted, jumped over grass tussocks and threw stones into pools of water. Then he challenged Two-Eyes to a race. "See that clump of trees," he said. "Last one there's a hairy hyena!" Off he ran as fast as he could. Two-Eyes was a bit slow on the uptake, and didn't realise it was a race at first. But when he did he shot off with all the advantage that four legs have over two. Littlenose might have just won, but Two-Eyes cheated. Just before he reached the trees something grabbed his ankle. Two-Eyes' trunk! And down he went in a heap, while Two-Eyes ran past and trumpeted in triumph.

"I'll pay you back for that," Littlenose shouted, then stopped. He had heard something. So had Two-Eyes. He stood with ears wide-spread, looking under the trees. Someone was crying.

Littlenose crept stealthily forward. There was a small clearing among the trees, and sitting in the grass and crying his heart out was a small boy. He looked much younger than Littlenose, and also vaguely familiar. He stopped crying when he saw Littlenose, and wiped the tears off his nose with the back of his hand. And Littlenose saw that the boy had a nose no bigger than his own. Not quite the same shape, but almost the same size. That was enough to make anyone weep.

"Are you hurt?" asked Littlenose. The boy said nothing for a moment, and when he did speak Littlenose couldn't understand a word of it. Littlenose repeated his question, but he still couldn't make sense of the reply. Probably from one of the tribes across the river, he thought. He knew that some of them spoke a different language from his own. He looked at the boy closely. He was on his feet by now, and didn't appear to be hurt.

"Did your father leave you here while he went hunting?" Littlenose tried again. "Mine did that too when I was your age. But *I* didn't cry. I expect he'll be back soon. Come and play. It'll help pass the time."

Even though they didn't speak each other's
language soon they were playing happily together.
They played hide and seek among the trees. Then
they threw stones at a stick stuck in the ground. It
was as they were getting really involved in a game of
bears and hunters that Littlenose's new friend
suddenly gave a shriek and dashed behind a tree.
Two-Eyes had at that moment come ambling into the
clearing to join in the fun, and the boy was terrified.
He gesticulated to Littlenose to run, and was
astonished when Littlenose put his arms round
Two-Eyes and said: "It's all right. It's Two-Eyes.
He's my friend, just the same as you are." The boy
took a lot of convincing, but in the end he reached out
a hand and timidly stroked Two-Eyes' trunk.

It was then that Littlenose realised that he was hungry, and took his picnic out of the hunting bag. The little boy watched, and licked his lips. "Don't you have any food?" asked Littlenose. "My father always left me something. You'd better share mine." He divided the meat and the honeycomb, and they each had an apple. Two-Eyes ate grass.

When they had eaten, they lay back in the long grass and rested, while Littlenose kept his ears cocked for the sound of a returning hunting party and the boy's father. But the afternoon wore on, and soon Littlenose could tell from the sun that it was time for him to set out for home. He waited a little longer, then stood up and said, "Well, we have to go now. It was nice meeting you, but it can't be long now before your father comes back, and then you can go home too. Goodbye."

Littlenose and Two-Eyes went off through the trees, but they had taken no more than a dozen steps when, with a loud wail, the new friend burst into tears, and ran after Littlenose and dragged at his furs.

Littlenose pulled free and said: "I have to go home now."

The boy cried even louder, and very slowly it began to dawn on Littlenose that no one was coming back for him. He hadn't been left to wait for his father. He was lost! That was why he had been crying to begin with.

Littlenose thought a bit longer. Then he said: "You can't stay here all night. You'd better come home with me." He took the little boy's hand, and set off once more for the cave.

Father was out at a hunters' meeting when they arrived, and Mother was still bustling about with odds and ends of spring cleaning. Littlenose said, "This is my new friend. He's lost, and I thought he could stay here till we find out where he comes from."

"Yes dear," said Mother without looking up from her work. "There's a cold snack over there. Help yourself, then straight to bed with you. It's late."

The two boys ate their cold supper, and then, rather than bother Mother again, Littlenose beckoned to his new friend, and led him to the back of the cave and his own special corner. He spread out the fur covers to go over both of them, then they both snuggled down. Littlenose fell asleep feeling slightly relieved. He had expected trouble when he came home with a strange child to spend the night.

The trouble came next morning, and couldn't have been worse if he had brought home a sabre-tooth tiger! Father sat down to breakfast, and Mother said, "Before you start, would you have a look and see if the boys are awake."

"*Boys!*" exclaimed Father in surprise.

"Yes, dear," said Mother. "Littlenose and his friend. He stayed the night."

At that moment, the boys, wakened by the voices, appeared rubbing their eyes. "Is breakfast ready?" asked Littlenose.

Father took one look at the stranger and started carrying on as if he were indeed a sabre-tooth tiger. He jumped up and down and shouted and waved his arms, then rushed out of the cave. He was back almost immediately. He pointed at the small stranger, who looked ready to burst into tears all over again, and shouted, "Don't move! Don't set foot outside of this cave!"

"What's he done?" asked Littlenose.

"It's what *you've* done," exclaimed Father. "And what he is. Where did you find him?"

"Over the hill, among some trees," said Littlenose. "He was lost. We waited for his people to come for him."

"Just as well for you that they didn't," said Father. "He's a Straightnose!" Littlenose gulped. Of course, that's why the little boy had a small nose. He wasn't just another boy with a little nose. Father went on. "The country will be crawling with Straightnose search parties looking for him, and here he is right in our midst. What will happen if they find him here I shudder to think!"

At that moment there was a shout from outside. A crowd had gathered, led by the Old Man. "I have declared a state of emergency," he announced. "There are two things to be done. First, we must conceal our presence here, in case the Straightnoses follow his trail; and second, we must try and return him to his own people. You know what has to be done."

He had barely finished speaking before cooking
fires were extinguished, everything was carried into
the caves, and the Neanderthal tribe began rolling
boulders to both conceal and barricade the cave
entrances. Meanwhile, Father was talking very
sternly to Littlenose. "This is all your fault," he said.
"So you will have to help put it right. We must take
the Straightnose boy back to where you found him so
that he can rejoin his own tribe."

It sounded dangerous but straightforward. And it turned out to be neither. Father, Littlenose, Two-Eyes and the Straightnose boy set off, keeping a sharp look-out for a possible search party. But they saw no one. They reached the clump of trees . . . and it was deserted. Father left them and scouted around, but there were neither signs nor tracks of Straightnoses. "We'll rest here," he said. "But we still must keep a good look-out. You take first watch, Littlenose." Littlenose climbed a tree from which he had a good view. But there was nothing to be seen but rolling grass-land and the occasional tree.

Then he thought he saw a movement a long way off. He looked again and waited. Yes, a line of tiny specks had appeared on the horizon. Men, moving in his direction. It must be a Straightnose search party. Littlenose called down to Father, who pulled himself up into the tree to see for himself. "Right," he said. "This is it. They're headed in this direction. We haven't much time."

Father jumped to the ground and took the little
Straightnose boy by the hand and led him to the spot
where Littlenose said he had found him. "Stay here
and don't move," he said. "They'll be here soon to
take you home." Then with Littlenose and Two-Eyes
he hurried away from the clump of trees in the
opposite direction to the Straightnoses. They paused

to rest hidden behind a bush, and looked back to see what would happen. The Straightnoses were still out of sight, and Father looked round to check that no one was missing. Yes, there was Littlenose and Two-Eyes and the little boy. THE LITTLE BOY?

"He followed us," said Littlenose. "He doesn't want us to leave him."

"What he wants has nothing to do with it," said Father in exasperation. And he grabbed the boy by the hand and ran, dragging him along behind him, back to the trees. But as soon as he turned to rejoin Littlenose, the small Straightnose began to cry again, and ran after him. The search party was getting dangerously close, within earshot probably; there was nothing else for Father to do but pick up the howling child and run like the wind for the safety of the bush.

Father and Littlenose watched as the searchers disappeared among the trees and emerged on the other side. "What do we do now?" asked Littlenose.

"I'll tell you what we are going to do," said Father. "We are going to follow the Straightnoses back to

their camp, wherever it is, and deliver this little horror to his own fireside." And without wasting another moment he rose to his feet and led the way along the trail of the Straightnoses. By late afternoon they had lost sight of the Straightnoses, but as darkness fell the glow of dozens of campfires could be seen straight ahead. The Straightnose camp proved to be a big one, with a great bustle of people moving among the tents and cooking fires. For a long time Father examined the scene. "Well, one thing's for sure. We're not going to walk straight in and say: 'Here's your boy'."

"I thought they'd be pleased to see us," said Littlenose. "We might get a reward."

"A bang on the head from a stone axe, more likely," said Father. "Let's wait, and see if we can think of a plan."

It was late into the night before anyone thought of
a plan. And it was Littlenose. The camp fires had
died down and the Straightnoses were all in their
tents, asleep. Littlenose pointed to the little boy. He
was also asleep. Curled up in the grass, with his
thumb in his mouth. Littlenose pointed to the boy
and to the sleeping camp. Father nodded and picked
up the boy. Hearts in their mouths, they picked their
way carefully into the camp. Snores came from some
of the tents, otherwise there was not a sound. A pile of
furs was lying by one of the smouldering fires, and
Father laid the little boy on them and tucked him in.
They looked down at him for a moment, then
Littlenose fumbled in his secret pocket of his furs and
took out his lucky coloured stone. He put it in the
little boy's hand, and thought, "I wish we could have
kept him. He would have made a good brother."

Then he and Father crept as quietly as they had come, back to where Two-Eyes was waiting. It was almost morning. The sky was growing bright and a few birds were singing. Littlenose turned for a last look at the Straightnose camp. People were coming out of the tents. Men were chopping wood. Women were preparing breakfast. Suddenly a great shout went up, and a crowd began to gather at one of the fires. A Straightnose man and a lady pushed through to the front, and Littlenose suddenly realised that he was crying as he saw the lady holding his little Straightnose friend in her arms. Then she turned and went with him into one of the tents.

Littlenose wiped his eyes, as Father in a curiously hoarse voice said, "Come on. Time we made ourselves scarce."

And they set off on the long trek back to their own cave where Mother and breakfast were waiting.

Littlenose the Dancer

It was a bitterly cold day in the depth of winter. The snow lay in great drifts around the caves of the Neanderthal folk, and they huddled close to their fires trying to ignore the draughts that were part of living in caves and passing the time by eating, sleeping, or whatever happened to be their favourite occupation. Father's favourite occupation was laying down the law, and he was doing it now with great gusto to Mother. Mother went on quietly with her mending, nodding her head from time to time to keep Father happy. Littlenose played one of his own complicated games in a corner, half listening.

"It's not a bit like it was in my young day," Father was saying. Nothing is, thought Littlenose. "I remember when the Sun Dance *meant* something.

Now it's just an excuse for a lot of singing and dancing and carrying on. It's for children.''

"Why do you go, then?" asked Mother. "Littlenose, these furs are quite worn through. I don't know how you do it."

"For the children's sake," replied Father, "and because it's expected of me."

Mother sewed for a moment, then said, "But the children don't take part. It's the hunters who do all the dancing and singing. What do you think, Littlenose?"

Littlenose knew that whatever he thought was bound to be wrong, so he mumbled vaguely without looking up. "That's what I think," said Mother.

"Hmph!" said Father. But he sat for a long time thinking about what Mother had said, and gradually the idea became less ridiculous. The preparations for the Sun Dance were getting under way, and the Old Man, leader of the tribe, had called a meeting for the following day to tie up loose ends. Father wondered if he dare suggest Mother's idea.

The Sun Dance was, of course, one of the most important events in the Neanderthal year. It was the great mid-winter festival held to encourage the sun to come back for another summer. And so far it had worked. It was also a super party, with eating and drinking and a decorated tree from which everyone got a present. It took a lot of organising, and that was why the Old Man had called a meeting in his cave of all the hunters. The meeting was drawing to a close, and the Old Man looked around him. "Before we adjourn," he said, "is there any other competent business?"

And Father, not giving himself time to change his mind, jumped to his feet and blurted out: "What about having children this year?"

"Eh?" said the Old Man. Everyone looked at Father as he went very red and continued: "It seems a shame not to let the young ones take part. They could do one of the ceremonial dances."

There was a moment of stunned silence. Then the Old Man said: "But it's never been done before."

"There must be a first time for everything," replied Father, amazed at his own boldness.

The assembled hunters shuffled their feet uncomfortably. Nothing worried a Neanderthal man more than novelty and change. The Old Man spoke again. "On the face of it it seems all right. But what will the rest of the tribe think?"

"Let's ask them," said Father. "And if everyone is in agreement we can meet again to work out details."

Not only was the tribe in agreement, everyone was wildly enthusiastic, particularly those with children. The Old Man held another meeting, and it was decided that the apprentice hunters would perform a dance for the entertainment of the grown-ups at the Sun Dance, which was just over a week away. Only boys, of course, would take part. The Old Man was firm on this. "Woman's place is in the cave," he said. "That is a law of nature. They are lucky to be allowed to watch! If we let them take part, there's no knowing where it will end." And that was that.

The training of the dance troupe was put in the hands of an elderly retired hunter who knew more about Neanderthal dances than anyone, and he immediately set about auditioning among the boys of the tribe. But, if the grown-ups were enthusiastic, the boys were anything but. They were dragged to the audition by their parents, and the unsuccessful ones went away grinning, ignoring the occasional cuff on the ear from disappointed mothers and fathers. Littlenose was selected . . . and threatened to run away from home. By the time that Father had dragged him, struggling, back to the cave he had gone off the whole thing. "It's all your fault," he shouted at Mother. "You and your stupid ideas about children and the Sun Dance!"

"I didn't go rushing off telling the Old Man," retorted Mother.

Father cuffed Littlenose in exasperation. "We'll have no more nonsense," he said. "You will dance, and you will dance properly. That's an order. From me, and from the Old Man."

Rehearsals started without delay. The Dancing Master selected a forest clearing some way from the caves which had only a thin covering of snow. Here the boys assembled and got their instructions. "We will rehearse and rehearse until it hurts," said the Dancing Master. "Then we will rehearse some more. You will learn your steps and practise them until I tell you to stop. You will think about them while you

eat, and dream about them while you sleep. And you will tell no one what we are doing. It is to be a secret only to be revealed at the Sun Dance. And you'll have fun."

"Who's he trying to fool," thought Littlenose.

Then they began. A basic step, the Dancing Master called it. Littlenose felt as if he had three left feet, and with the other boys he tripped and stumbled while the Dancing Master stood on a flat rock and beat the time with a long black staff. Day after day it went on. Littlenose ached all over. He barely managed to finish his evening meal before he collapsed into bed to dream about dancing. The basic steps were soon accompanied by arm movements and body movements. Father and Mother asked him about the rehearsals, but he just grunted and said it was a secret. So they left him alone.

But there was someone determined not to leave Littlenose alone. And that was Two-Eyes, who wanted to play with Littlenose as usual. Every morning Littlenose went off on his own. The little mammoth watched him disappear into the forest but soon lost sight of him among the trees. He wandered about disconsolately, getting in everyone's way, so that he was shouted at and chased away by all the tribe. The Old Man, however, realised how lonely he must be without Littlenose, and took to stroking him and patting his short furry trunk. One day he gave Two-Eyes an apple, which Two-Eyes, being a mammoth and rather like an elephant, didn't forget.

Meanwhile the preparations for the Sun Dance were well under way. A clearing had been swept clear of snow, and the surrounding trees hung with garlands of evergreens. A tall spruce tree had been set up in the clearing and was almost ready with its coloured berry decorations and carefully wrapped presents. No one talked of anything else but the coming Sun Dance, and particularly the dance to be performed by the apprentice hunters. What would it be, they wondered. The Great Elk? The Dance of the Woolly Mammoths? The Hunters and the Bears?

But it was none of these. One morning the boys assembled as usual, and the Dancing Master stepped on to his rock and said: "Now, here is the news you have all been waiting for."

"The dance has been cancelled," said Littlenose.

"Don't be impertinent, boy," said the Master. "No, I can now reveal which dance we will present for the entertainment of the tribe. It is the Dance of the Birds. Isn't that lovely?"

The boys tried to look as if it was.

The Dancing Master now went round his troupe and gave each boy the name of a bird. One was a thrush. One a gull. Another a sparrow. When he got to Littlenose he paused. "I have a special role for you, Littlenose," he said. "No one else will do." Littlenose wondered if perhaps he was teasing. "You, Littlenose, shall be the eagle, king of the sky."

Littlnose glowed with pride. He couldn't have been so bad after all.

Then they were told the story which the dance portrayed. It was all very complicated, and didn't make much sense to Littlenose, and he was still trying to puzzle it out when the Dancing Master sprang back on to his rock and cried: "Places, everybody!" Then he called out the time: "A-one, a-two, a-one, two, three, four." And off they went into yet another rehearsal. But now it was somehow different. Littlenose found it much less tiring and his legs didn't ache so much. It was even, strangely, almost *fun*. The Master spent less time shouting, and simply stood beating the time on the rock with the end of his staff. Of course there was no music. That would be provided on the night by the crowd singing and clapping their hands, but even so, the dance carried Littlenose along until he almost believed that he really was the eagle, king of the air.

Now, no Neanderthal dance was complete without a costume of some sort, and no one had said anything about costumes to the boys, but one evening, just as they were going home, the Dancing Master said, "Come to my cave tomorrow. We have something to take into the forest with us. And when they did meet at the cave, they found the floor strewn with skin-covered bundles, one for each boy. The master pointed out which were whose, and carrying them carefully they set off for rehearsal. As they expected, these were the costumes. "We must be very careful," said the Dancing Master. "They're pretty old, and I've had to take them in to fit. The feathers are coming loose in places."

The costumes were imitation wings which were
worn on the arms, and feathered head-dresses.
Littlenose was last to unpack his because of a tight
knot, and as he did so, the Dancing Master said,
"Now you'll see why only you could be the eagle."
Instead of a head-dress, Littlenose's costume had a
magnificent eagle mask, with a curved beak. "You're
the only one it would fit."

Littlenose almost cried. He had been given his
name because his nose was no bigger than a berry,
and not big and snuffly like a real Neanderthal nose.
Whoever the mask had first been made for must have
had a small nose. Blinking back tears, Littlenose
pulled the mask over his head. He turned to the other
boys, and they fell back a step. It didn't matter about
his nose. *He* was the eagle, king of the sky. Then he
put on the wings and waited for the word to start
rehearsal.

The day of the Sun Dance came at last. As the tribe assembled in the clearing by the decorated tree there was an eager buzz of conversation all around. The proceedings started with a dance by the hunters, but no one was really interested, and people chattered to their friends without paying much attention. They were anxious to see the long-awaited performance by the apprentice hunters. At length, when the audience was almost bursting with impatience, the Old Man stepped forward and announced: "And now, the moment we've all been waiting for. A big hand, ladies and gentlemen, for the Dance of the Birds!"

Under the trees, beyond the torch-light, the Dancing Master said: "You're on. Good luck!" And the boys, led by Littlenose, leapt out in front of the audience and into their routine. And the crowd loved it. They clapped and cheered. They stamped their feet to the rhythm as the boys skipped and pirouetted, and the torch-light gleamed on the feather costumes and particularly on Littlenose's eagle mask with the curved beak. Littlenose was enjoying himself. He put all he had into his part, and at the same time tried to see through the eye holes in the mask for a glimpse of Father and Mother. He couldn't make them out. But he did see something else. For a moment the light had caught a pair of eyes. Mammoth eyes. Small. One red and one green. It could only be Two-Eyes. What was he doing here?

Two-Eyes, of course, was looking for Littlenose. He had missed him over the past week, and wanted to play. And now he had found him. In the middle of what appeared to be a most enjoyable game. Without more ado, Two-Eyes pushed through the crowd, and trumpeting happily ran to join Littlenose.

Littlenose was horrified. What should he do? Run? Grab Two-Eyes? But he remembered how often the Dancing Master had said *the show must go on* and *you mustn't let your public down.* He decided to ignore Two-Eyes but this was easier said than done. He led the dancers around and behind Two-Eyes. He ducked and dodged. But Two-Eyes was not to be shaken off. In desperation, Littlenose made a grab at Two-Eyes. He wasn't sure what he was trying to do, but with great difficulty because of his eagle's wings he hauled himself on to Two-Eyes' back. And Two-Eyes raced round and round the Sun Dance tree with the other dancers in hot pursuit in a trail of flying feathers. The audience cheered and laughed until the tears rolled down their cheeks, while the Dancing Master leaned against a tree and sobbed, "What are they trying to do to me?"

Suddenly Two-Eyes stopped. He had seen a familiar figure. It was the Old Man. He had befriended him when he was lonely. And now he ran towards him. Littlenose desperately tried to keep his balance with his feather-clad arms outstretched, and the audience cheered as Two-Eyes stopped in front of the Old Man, trunk raised, and Littlenose sat erect on his back looking every bit the king of the air. And that was the end of the dance. The other dancers had since given up. But it didn't matter. The whole troupe was treated like heroes for the rest of the Sun Dance.

Next day, the Old Man sent for the Dancing Master. "Training boys I thought would be hard enough," he said. "But a *mammoth*! Trade secret, I suppose."

The Dancing Master said, "Sort of," and went away muttering to himself. He had earlier planned to do something about Littlenose, like feeding him to a sabre-tooth tiger, but now decided to leave well alone.

Mother basked in the glory of the whole affair, and said she hoped that Littlenose would dance the following year. But as he snuggled under his furs in bed, Littlenose made up his mind that even if they asked him to play a whole herd of mammoths he would never dance again. And with that he fell asleep.

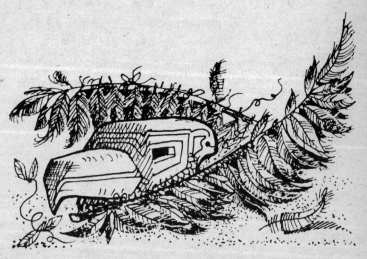

Was it really fun being a Neanderthal boy?

Littlenose didn't go to school. He went fishing. He went on picnics. And he played games with Two-Eyes. But, was it all that marvellous being one of the Neanderthal folk?

To begin with, we don't call their time the Ice Age for nothing. The summers were only *just* warm, and the winters were colder than we can imagine. And the caves they called home probably felt cold, damp and draughty. And suppose they fell sick or had an accident? Well, the Doctor and Auntie would do their best, and from bones found in the caves it seems that even a little brain surgery was not beyond the Neanderthal medicine man! But probably many a poor Neanderthal person was carried away by nothing more serious than a cold in the head.

And all the excitement! Do you sometimes get bored going to school every day? Would you really prefer to only just escape a sabre-tooth tiger or an enraged bison, or to hide trembling in the bushes until the dreaded Straightnoses had passed by? All this happened to Littlenose.

Perhaps Littlenose would be happier living today. What do you think?

100,000 YEARS AGO people wore no clothes. They lived in caves and hunted animals for food. They were called NEANDERTHAL.

50,000 YEARS AGO when Littlenose lived, clothes were made out of fur. But now there were other people. Littlenose called them Straightnoses. Their proper name is HOMO SAPIENS.

5,000 YEARS AGO there were no Neanderthal people left. People wore cloth as well as fur. They built in wood and stone. They grew crops and kept cattle.

1,000 YEARS AGO towns were built, and men began to travel far from home by land and sea to explore the world.

500 YEARS AGO towns became larger, as did the ships in which men travelled. The houses they built were very like those we see today.

100 YEARS AGO people used machines to do a lot of the harder work. They could now travel by steam train. Towns and cities became very big, with factories as well as houses.

TODAY we don't hunt for our food, but buy it in shops. We travel by car and aeroplane. Littlenose would not understand any of this. Would YOU like to live as Littlenose did?

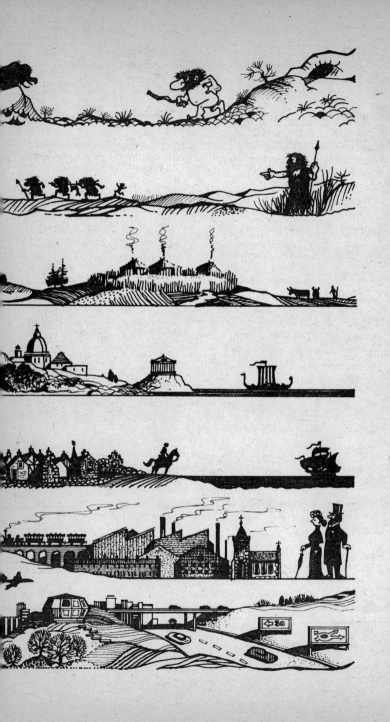